Dear Reader,

As parents we search for ways to engage our kids in rich learning experiences that expand their horizons and help them develop their own passions and interests.

Reading is one of the most powerful ways to open new worlds for a child. When we read a book, we teach children essential vocabulary, creativity, and problem solving skills through the context of a story.

Unfortunately, not every child receives one-to-one attention reading with an adult.

Currently, one third of America's children are entering school without the basic, fundamental skills they need.[1]

That's why we are participating in Jumpstart's Read for the Record campaign, a national initiative to raise awareness of the importance of early childhood education by setting a world record for the greatest number of children reading with an adult on the same day.

By joining Jumpstart's Read for the Record campaign, not only do you foster a love of reading with children close to you, you also support Jumpstart's work to bring this same one-to-one attention to children in low-income communities across the country.

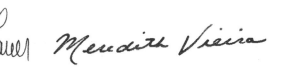

The proceeds from this book enable Jumpstart to reach more underserved children to prepare them for kindergarten and, ultimately, for life.

Join us by reading with a child in your life through Jumpstart's Read for the Record campaign. Together we can break a world record and **make early education a national priority.**

Sincerely,

Matt Lauer *Meredith Vieira*

1. Landry, S. (2005). Chapter 6: Content Areas. *Effective Early Childhood Programs: Turning Knowledge into Action.*

i

I believe in the power of reading

I thank my grandparents and mother for instilling in me a true love of reading, and for encouraging me to express myself.

When I was growing up, my grandparents and mother provided love and support when times were rough. By the time I was eleven, I was writing rhymes and creating music.

Now that I'm a parent, I know the most important gift I can give my children is the gift of empowerment through reading. Every child needs someone to help unlock his or her potential, and reading is the master key. By spending time with my children every day, I show them that I believe in them, just as my grandparents and mother believed in me.

I believe in Jumpstart, because it kindles the spirit of dreaming in preschool children in low-income communities and has a lifelong positive effect. When Jumpstart children read with adults, they learn the importance of literacy and language, and they learn social skills that will benefit them for the rest of their lives.

Join me in Jumpstart's Read for the Record campaign as we come together to celebrate the power of reading.

LL Cool J is a talented entertainer, actor, author, recording artist, two-time Grammy Award winner, and NAACP Image Award winner.

What is Jumpstart?

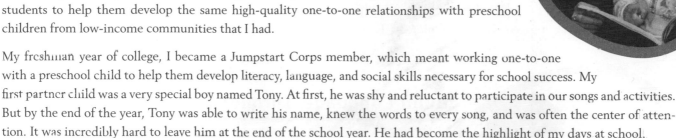

Hi, I am Amanda Natalle and I am a Jumpstart Corps alumna and am currently employed by Jumpstart at the University of Pittsburgh. When I entered college, I didn't know where my life was going or what I wanted to do with it. Volunteering for Jumpstart provided three years of constant inspiration as I watched the children I worked with grow to become enthusiastic learners. After graduation, I became a site manager at Jumpstart Pittsburgh and now mentor college students to help them develop the same high-quality one-to-one relationships with preschool children from low-income communities that I had.

My freshman year of college, I became a Jumpstart Corps member, which meant working one-to-one with a preschool child to help them develop literacy, language, and social skills necessary for school success. My first partner child was a very special boy named Tony. At first, he was shy and reluctant to participate in our songs and activities. But by the end of the year, Tony was able to write his name, knew the words to every song, and was often the center of attention. It was incredibly hard to leave him at the end of the school year. He had become the highlight of my days at school.

Talk to any Jumpstart Corps member, and they will tell you the many reasons they volunteer for Jumpstart. You do it for the Saturday service projects with your team. You do it for the three-hour conversations with the staff after everyone else has gone home. You do it for the friendships in your Corps. But most of all, you do it for the children—for their smiles, their hugs, their endless appreciation of your presence in their lives. And you do it for yourself. Because only an organization like Jumpstart could teach you that you have the ability to change the world and the lives around you.

What is Jumpstart's Read for the Record?

Jumpstart's Read for the Record is a national campaign to connect adults and children in the powerful learning relationships that every child needs before entering kindergarten. When you take part in Jumpstart's Read for the Record, you are advocating for the importance of quality early childhood education and the promise that all young children bring to the world. Because 100 percent of the proceeds fund our work with at-risk children, when you purchase this book, you give an invaluable gift to a Jumpstart child: precious time with a trained and caring mentor.

Last year more than 258,000 children around the world participated in Jumpstart's Read for the Record campaign by reading the same book with an adult on the same day in libraries, classrooms, homes, stores, and parent groups. This year, on October 2, we need your help to connect even more children and adults in the powerful learning relationships that model Jumpstart's work in classrooms every day.

In addition to reading the classic children's tale *Corduroy* with a child in your life, Jumpstart hopes that you will engage your family and friends in Jumpstart's Read for the Record. Together, we can make early education a national priority!

Visit **www.readfortherecord.org** to discover additional ways to support Jumpstart.

Make the Most of Reading Together

Remember these simple ways to share the joy of reading with your child:

- Set aside time to read every day. Create a special time and place for reading.
- Make reading fun and interactive. Be playful and enjoy it!
- Have a conversation. Explain new words and ask questions.
- Read the book again! Your child learns more each time you reread a story.

Build Language Through Reading

Stories hold endless potential to develop a child's imagination and help build a greater understanding of the world. Take time to explain new words in the story by providing a simple definition. Help make the words that describe Corduroy's adventures in the department store familiar to your child. For example:

- **Customers**—the people who come to a store to buy things.
- **Department store**—a big store with many different areas where you can buy clothing and things for your home, like sheets, pillows, beds, couches, pots, pans, toasters, and more.
- **Searching**—looking very carefully for something.
- **Escalator**—stairs that move to take you from one floor to another.
- **Yanked**—pulled or jerked very hard.
- **Night watchman**—someone who guards a place at night when it is closed.
- **Piggy bank**—a container used to save money until you want to buy something.

To find more words to explore with your child, visit **www.readfortherecord.org**.

Making Reading a Conversation

As you read, each page provides opportunities for you to talk with your child. Conversations strengthen listening and speaking skills. Here are some examples for you to try at home:

Page 13

After reading the page, point to the picture and say, "Look at Corduroy riding up the _____." Pause to see if your child recalls the word *escalator*. If not, you can remind the child. "He thinks he is climbing a mountain. Have you ever been on an escalator? Was it fun? Where did it go?"

Page 17

Before reading this page, pause and comment, "I wonder what Corduroy is doing? Why? Hmmm, what do you think will happen next?"

Page 32

Ask your child, "What do you think Corduroy and Lisa will do next now that they are friends? What would you do with Corduroy if he were your friend?"

Beyond the Story

Read it again! If it isn't already, *Corduroy* will fast become a favorite story for your child. He or she will want to read it again and again. Each time, your child will absorb more from the story and continue to build knowledge about the world.

Let's talk! Children love to retell stories and connect them to their own lives. Here are some fun and easy things you can do to connect the story of *Corduroy* to your child's life.

- **Visit a department store.** The next time you head to the mall or a department store, ask questions to help your child recall the story of *Corduroy*. Ride the escalator. Find the mattress department.

- **Change sheets together.** When you change the bedding, invite your child to help. Take the sheets off and look at the mattress. Are there buttons on it like in the story of *Corduroy*?

- **Make up new adventures.** Corduroy used to live with the other dolls and animals in the toy department. They were all waiting for someone to come and take them home. Look back at the first few pages of the book with your child. Who might be next to find a new home? What kind of adventure will that toy have when someone takes it home?

- **Everybody has a cuddly friend growing up.** Did you have a favorite teddy bear? Tell your child about it. Even better, dig out an old photograph, if you have one!

Go to **www.readfortherecord.org** to find more activities and to share your ideas for Corduroy's next adventure!

CORDUROY

CORDUROY

Story and Pictures by Don Freeman

THE VIKING PRESS / NEW YORK

To Sally Elizabeth Kildow
and Patrick Steven Duff Kildow,
who know how a bear feels about buttons

VIKING
Published by Penguin Group
Penguin Young Readers Group, 345 Hudson Street, New York, New York 10014, U.S.A.
Penguin Group (Canada), 90 Eglinton Avenue East, Suite 700, Toronto, Ontario, Canada M4P 2Y3 (a division of Pearson Penguin Canada Inc.)
Penguin Books Ltd, 80 Strand, London WC2R 0RL, England
Penguin Ireland, 25 St Stephen's Green, Dublin 2, Ireland (a division of Penguin Books Ltd)
Penguin Group (Australia), 250 Camberwell Road, Camberwell, Victoria 3124, Australia (a division of Pearson Australia Group Pty Ltd)
Penguin Books India Pvt Ltd, 11 Community Centre, Panchsheel Park, New Delhi – 110 017, India
Penguin Group (NZ), 67 Apollo Drive, Rosedale, North Shore 0632, New Zealand (a division of Pearson New Zealand Ltd.)
Penguin Books (South Africa) (Pty) Ltd, 24 Sturdee Avenue, Rosebank, Johannesburg 2196, South Africa

Penguin Books Ltd, Registered Offices: 80 Strand, London WC2R 0RL, England

Corduroy first published in 1968 by The Viking Press
This special edition published in 2008 by Viking, a division of Penguin Young Readers Group

1   3   5   7   9   10   8   6   4   2

Corduroy Library of Congress catalog card number: 77-71209

This edition ISBN 978-0-670-01111-7

Manufactured in China

Corduroy is a bear who once lived in the toy department of a big store. Day after day he waited with all the other animals and dolls for somebody to come along and take him home.

The store was always filled with shoppers buying all sorts of things,
but no one ever seemed to want a small bear in green overalls.

Then one morning a little girl stopped and looked straight into
Corduroy's bright eyes.

"Oh, Mommy!" she said. "Look! There's the very bear I've always
wanted."

"Not today, dear." Her mother sighed. "I've spent too much already.
Besides, he doesn't look new. He's lost the button to one of his
shoulder straps."

Corduroy watched them sadly as they walked away.

"I didn't know I'd lost a button," he said to himself. "Tonight I'll go and see if I can find it."

Late that evening, when all the shoppers had gone and the doors
were shut and locked, Corduroy climbed carefully down from his

shelf and began searching everywhere on the floor for his lost
button.

Suddenly he felt the floor moving under him! Quite by accident he had stepped onto an escalator—and up he went!

"Could this be a mountain?" he wondered. "I think I've always wanted to climb a mountain."

He stepped off the escalator as it reached the next floor, and there, before his eyes, was a most amazing sight—

14

tables and chairs and lamps and sofas, and rows and rows of beds.
"This must be a palace!" Corduroy gasped. "I guess I've always
wanted to live in a palace."

He wandered around admiring the furniture.
"This must be a bed," he said. "I've always wanted to sleep in a
bed." And up he crawled onto a large, thick mattress.

All at once he saw something small and round.
"Why, here's my button!" he cried. And he tried to pick it up. But,
like all the other buttons on the mattress, it was tied down tight.

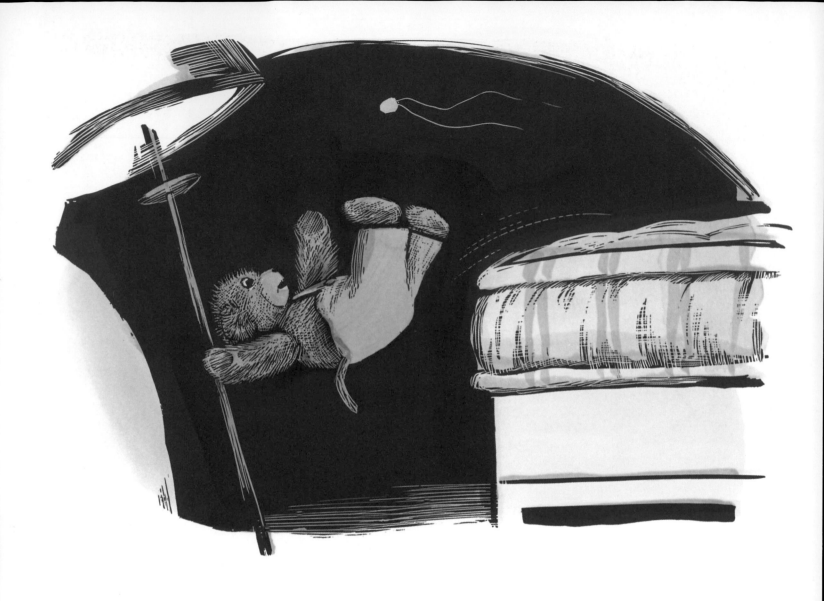

He yanked and pulled with both paws until POP! Off came the button—and off the mattress Corduroy toppled,

bang into a tall floor lamp. Over it fell with a crash!

Corduroy didn't know it, but there was someone else awake in the store. The night watchman was going his rounds on the floor above. When he heard the crash he came dashing down the escalator.

"Now who in the world did that!" he exclaimed. "Somebody must be hiding around here!"

He flashed his light under and over sofas and beds until he came to
the biggest bed of all. And there he saw two fuzzy brown ears
sticking up from under the cover.

"Hello!" he said. "How did *you* get upstairs?"

The watchman tucked Corduroy under his arm and carried him
down the escalator

and set him on the shelf in the toy department with the other
animals and dolls.

Corduroy was just waking up when the first customers came into
the store in the morning. And there, looking at him with a wide,
warm smile, was the same little girl he'd seen only the day before.

"I'm Lisa," she said, "and you're going to be my very own bear. Last night I counted what I've saved in my piggy bank and my mother said I could bring you home."

"Shall I put him in a box for you?" the saleslady asked.

"Oh, no thank you," Lisa answered. And she carried Corduroy home in her arms.

28

She ran all the way up four flights of stairs, into her family's apartment, and straight to her own room.

Corduroy blinked. There was a chair and a chest of drawers, and alongside a girl-size bed stood a little bed just the right size for him. The room was small, nothing like that enormous palace in the department store.

"This must be home," he said. "I *know* I've always wanted a home!"

Lisa sat down with Corduroy on her lap and began to sew a button
on his overalls.

"I like you the way you are," she said, "but you'll be more
comfortable with your shoulder strap fastened."

"You must be a friend," said Corduroy. "I've always wanted a friend."

"Me too!" said Lisa, and gave him a big hug.

ABOUT THIS BOOK

As we prepare to break the world record for the largest shared reading event ever, all of us at Jumpstart thank the people and businesses of Pearson, Sponsor and Founding Partner of Jumpstart's Read for the Record Campaign, for their continuing support.

This custom limited edition of the Viking children's classic *Corduroy* has been published and distributed by Pearson, ensuring that 100 percent of the proceeds from the sale of this book directly support Jumpstart's work with children from low-income communities across America.

In addition to underwriting this custom limited edition of *Corduroy*, Pearson and its people across the U.S. and around the world are taking part in Jumpstart's Read for the Record celebrations and working with governors, mayors, PTAs, schools, libraries, and local organizations to spread the word and highlight the importance and the power of reading. The Pearson Foundation is also providing more than 100,000 copies of *Corduroy* to at-risk children in school districts and community organizations worldwide.

Since 2001, Pearson businesses—Pearson Education, the Financial Times Group, and the Penguin Group—have shared Jumpstart's goal of ensuring that every child in America enters school prepared to succeed. Please find out more about the Pearson-Jumpstart Partnership and about all the ways that Pearson helps people around the world to live and learn by visiting **www.pearsonfoundation.org**.

jumpstart

CONNECT EARLY